Computer-linked
I've tinkered with
much that one of
days they're completely
going to fritz on me.

Twin blasters. Custom painted
of course. MandalTech Jai'galaar
models. They're sealed, so the
paint doesn't interfere
with any of the
workings.

MY
GEAR

Also, my **holo-imager!**
Whenever I travel somewhere new
I like to capture images of
beautiful things. Or sad things.
Or even ugly, angry things.
Basically, anything that makes me
FEEL! I'll probably put some
of my favorites in this
sketchbook.

Sure, I'm the saboteur for this happy band of rebels.

But in my heart I'm an ARTIST!

Here's a few of the art tools I have lying around my quarters. I'm always turning random stuff into new art tools - who says recycled objects can't be used as paint spreaders?

Here's my **FAVORITE** sprayer.

Load the paint canister inside and squeeze the trigger. It sprays the paint in a pressurized mist. It's really easy to control the width and intensity of your lines or to switch between colors.

Here's the DELUXE

paint sprayer. If it looks like a fire extinguisher, that's because it used to be one! This one is FOR OUTSIDE USE ONLY! It covers a LOT of area in a few seconds, and it's got a SENSITIVE trigger, too!

(Zeb found both these facts out the hard way. Poor Zeb—he was holding it backward too!)

Here's a handful of color sticks.

Good for drawing.

Here are some of my stencils. I use these when I want to make words or patterns consistently, and over and over again.

And HERE'S one of my respirators. Never want to work around paint fumes without a respirator. My Mando helmet has a respirator built in, but sometimes I feel like going with a lightweight option like this one.

SABINE

DETONATOR

And here are my favorite art tools of all: EXPLOSIVES

Nothing makes me smile quite as wide as when I blow something up that once belonged to the Empire.

Yes, I said ART tools. Detonators can be modified to release a spray of paint when they're triggered! And even the standard KA-BLAMMY detonators can make beautiful blasts!

Different substances make different colors when they explode, so I create capsules based on each substance's color. Sometimes I add more than one in a detonator shell so the explosions have more than one color. And then it's art!

So all you have to do is load the substances you want into mini capsules, pack them into the detonator shell so the blast will oxidize them in a specific order, and you're done!

CONGRATS, you're an artist!

BOOM!

I like to retrofit everyday containers to use as shells for explosives. Recycling is good! It also means fewer questions if an Imperial trooper happens to look my way.

Every explosive needs FUEL and a FUSE.

MY OWN RECIPE

Get fancy with fuel:
baradium, baradium nitrate, nergon-14, megonite

Get colorful with fuel:

Purple: rubidium

Orange: calcium

Green: barium

Yellow: sodium

Red: strontium

Gold: iron

Blue: copper

White: beryllium

Experiment with fuses: Countdown timer, thumb trigger, motion sensor, altitude sensor

Other explosives: Pros/Cons

Thermal detonators: Usually powered by a baradium core. Every fringe bounty hunter swears by these, but in most cases they're too overpowered for my tastes.

Rhydonium: Pretty volatile. Don't jostle it, don't get it too hot. Or cold. It's really a type of exotic starship fuel.

Detonite tape: My fave! This explosive also comes as putty, but I like the tape. Sticks to everything. Doesn't have quite the boom power as the other ones, but you can always just wad a bunch of detonite tape up into a giant ball.

We're nomads, but the Ghost is our HOME.

GHOST

She's a Corellian Engineering Corporation VCX-100 light freighter, but she's been modified. **A LOT.** Not just outside the hull, but also the engine, the shielding, and other mechanical upgrades that are easy to miss unless you know what to look for. Kind of like us, really! We may seem like a crew of star traders, but let us loose on the Empire and we'll show them what we can do.

Here's the nose laser turret. This turret is MINE! I added a hook on the seat so I can hang my helmet from it. I also started marking the instrument panel with a running tally, showing how many TIEs I've smoked since I signed on.

PRACTICE MAKES PERFECT

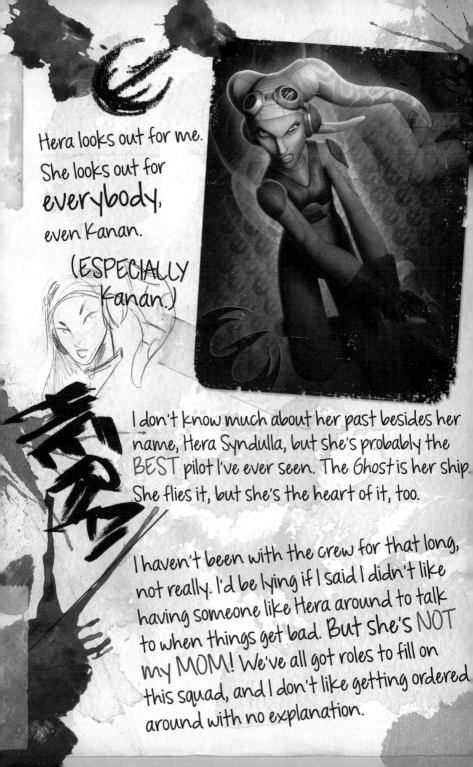

Hera looks out for me. She looks out for **everybody,** even Kanan.

(ESPECIALLY Kanan.)

I don't know much about her past besides her name, Hera Syndulla, but she's probably the BEST pilot I've ever seen. The Ghost is her ship. She flies it, but she's the heart of it, too.

I haven't been with the crew for that long, not really. I'd be lying if I said I didn't like having someone like Hera around to talk to when things get bad. But she's NOT my MOM! We've all got roles to fill on this squad, and I don't like getting ordered around with no explanation.

This section of the Ghost houses the Phantom, a speedy ship that can separate for missions of its own.

A thick hull and a good deflector shield generator come in handy in our line of work.

GHOST

HOME SWEET HOME

HERA

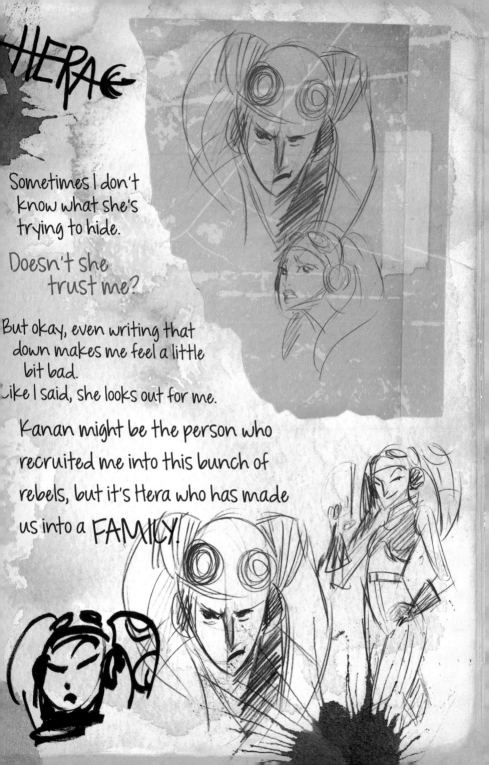

Sometimes I don't know what she's trying to hide.

Doesn't she trust me?

But okay, even writing that down makes me feel a little bit bad.

Like I said, she looks out for me.

Kanan might be the person who recruited me into this bunch of rebels, but it's Hera who has made us into a FAMILY!

My cabin? My studio!

Here's what my cabin looks like today, but I change things up a lot. Got to keep it DYNAMIC, you know?

I like to test out new themes.

Sometimes that means experimenting with new mediums of art. Just nothing explosive, septic, acidic, noxious, or stinky—

yeah yeah, I've got it, Hera!

I keep asking for permission to have a PET but nobody will let me keep one aboard the ship. What's the worst that could happen?

I mean, a pet can't possibly have a **WORSE** attitude than Chopper!

Or leave more fur lying around than Zeb!

ZEB

Zeb is like a big brother to me.

And when I say BIG I'm not messing around. Mr. Garazeb Orrelios is a muscle-packing Lasat who can tear a door from its hinges but who always knows to back off whenever I'm feeling down.

Okay, he's also a complete vacuum-brain. But I love the guy! I never let him near my art stuff though.

Or my detonators.

Or anything breakable.

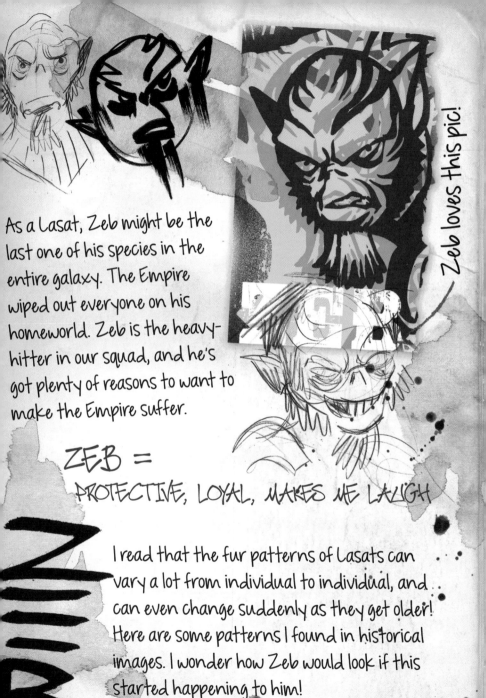

As a Lasat, Zeb might be the last one of his species in the entire galaxy. The Empire wiped out everyone on his homeworld. Zeb is the heavy-hitter in our squad, and he's got plenty of reasons to want to make the Empire suffer.

ZEB = PROTECTIVE, LOYAL, MAKES ME LAUGH

Zeb loves this pic!

I read that the fur patterns of Lasats can vary a lot from individual to individual, and can even change suddenly as they get older! Here are some patterns I found in historical images. I wonder how Zeb would look if this started happening to him!

Check out Chopper! I tolerate him, but I guess I've always had a soft spot for strays and mongrels.

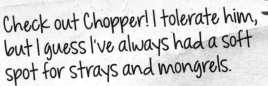

Chopper's numerical designation is C1-10P, but we like his nickname better. As an astromech droid, he basically works as the Ghost's engineer. Chopper calculates hyperspace coordinates and fixes our equipment when it breaks down.

The equipment breaks down a **LOT** around here. This is probably why Chopper has such a bad attitude!

Kanan, Hera and I are the only ones on board the Ghost who can understand Chopper's beeps and whistles. It's a good thing, too! You wouldn't believe what he says sometimes! The mouth on this little droid!

KANAN is the leader of our crew, and he's great at it. But let's get real for a second. Everybody knows nothing would get done without Hera.

But we love you Kanan!

Kanan has a Jedi background. I don't know much about that whole tradition, but I do know that he owns a lightsaber and he can move stuff with his mind a little.

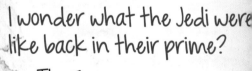

I wonder what the Jedi were like back in their prime?

The Empire has erased nearly all mention of them. Is Kanan a good example of what the Jedi were like? He would have been even younger than me back when the Empire took over...

What made the Jedi so special?

I mean, look at me—I can fly! Okay, okay, maybe if I had a jet pack. But I doubt any Jedi could do that!

BUT...then there's that whole "moving things without touching them" ability. If I could toss dye packets into the air with my mind and explode them on the sides of government skyscrapers, think of the beautiful canvases I could paint!

REBELS RULE
DEFEAT THE EMPIRE

KANAN

JEDI MASTER

We've made Lothal our cause.

INJUSTICE

And we **ARE** going to make a difference.

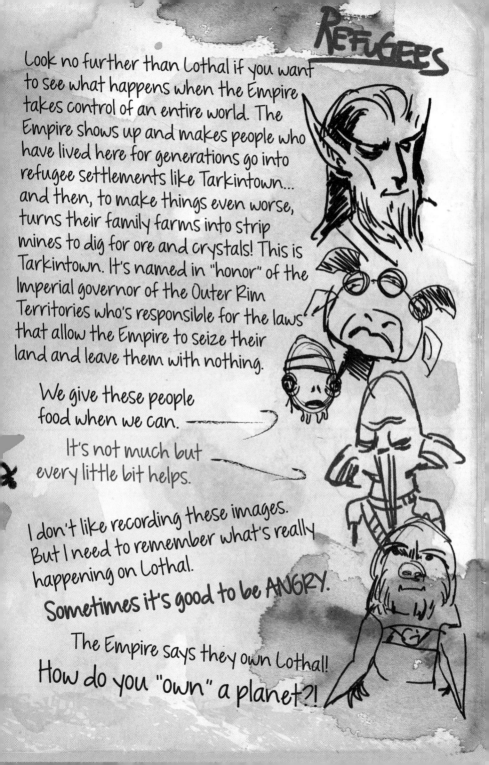

Look no further than Lothal if you want to see what happens when the Empire takes control of an entire world. The Empire shows up and makes people who have lived here for generations go into refugee settlements like Tarkintown... and then, to make things even worse, turns their family farms into strip mines to dig for ore and crystals! This is Tarkintown. It's named in "honor" of the Imperial governor of the Outer Rim Territories who's responsible for the laws that allow the Empire to seize their land and leave them with nothing.

We give these people food when we can.

It's not much but every little bit helps.

I don't like recording these images. But I need to remember what's really happening on Lothal.

Sometimes it's good to be ANGRY.

The Empire says they own Lothal! How do you "own" a planet?!

We completed a bunch of jobs recently and we're really getting in synch on how we operate.

Everything is coded now, to prevent the Empire from listening in on our transmissions. We're also setting up shadow sites. These are rendezvous points and supply drops scattered across the face of Lothal, but only we know where they are. So far the Empire is completely in the dark.

And here's who we're up against:

Commandant Aresko: Runs the Imperial Academy near Capital City. Thinks he runs the whole planet. I knew officers like Aresko when I attended the Imperial Academy on Mandalore. They love being arrogant.

Supply Master Lyste: Has a tight grip on all cargo shipments arriving at the Capital City starport. A big part of our job is to steal or blow up any cargo that might help the Empire, and Lyste has started boosting security. He's not a complete dummy.

Okay, based on recent happenings I had to go back to this page and add another two. As if we didn't have enough enemies!

Agent Kallus: Kallus is with the Imperial Security Bureau. It's bad that the ISB has gotten involved because Kallus has a lot more authority than the officers here on Lothal. But it's also great! Why? It means we're getting noticed, which means we're getting results!

The Inquisitor: A scary-deadly Force user. Like the bad version of a Jedi. I think they were called the Sith. So far Kanan hasn't said much about this guy. The Ghost hops around to other places in the sector, but we always come back to Lothal. We've got work to do.

Taskmaster Grint: He's Aresko's flunky. He's also an idiot. Mean-spirited, and he laughs when he hurts other beings.

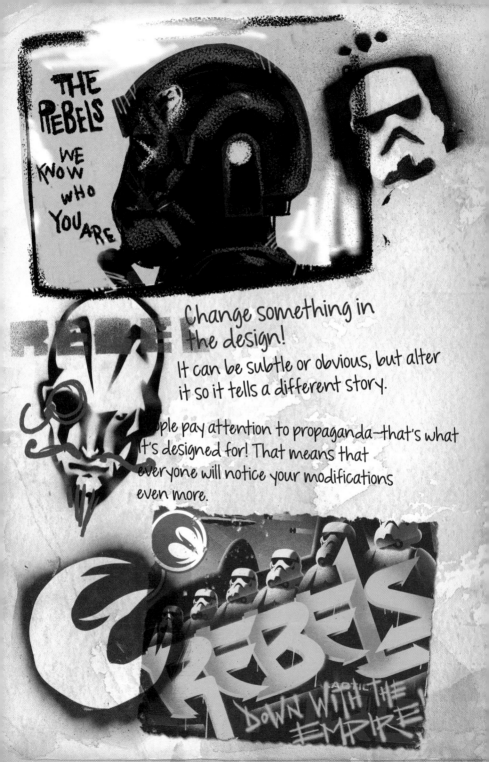

THE REBELS
WE KNOW WHO YOU ARE

Change something in the design!

It can be subtle or obvious, but alter it so it tells a different story.

People pay attention to propaganda—that's what it's designed for! That means that everyone will notice your modifications even more.

REBELS

DOWN WITH THE EMPIRE

"Defacement of Imperial property is a capital crime" according to Imperial Statute 342.

Well, you know what I have to say about THAT.

Here's a handbill they were passing out in Capital City, and here's how I'm marking it up.

IMPERIAL STATUTE 342—X0088

A. No Imperial citizen shall write, paint or draw any inscription, figure or mark of any type on any structure operated under the auspices of system, planetary, or local Imperial governmental jurisdiction.

B. No Imperial citizen shall carry an aerosol paint sprayer, [or] dye-burst canister, [or] indelible color stick, [or] etching acid into any building or other facility with the intent to violate the provisions of this statute.

C. Any Imperial citizen found to be in violation of this statute through the action of, or suspicion of, etching, drawing, carving, sketching, engraving, or otherwise altering, changing, or impairing the physical integrity of any structural surface will be arrested and incarcerated indefinitely without recourse of a judicial trial.

I hope that when people in Capital City see these kinds of examples they'll start doing the same thing. The Empire only has authority when people BELIEVE that they do!

REBEL

Art has power,
and the Empire gets it.

I've been studying
Imperial propaganda.

Look at these
posters!
There's some genuine talent
behind these pictures and
that iconography.

But it's all mass-produced.

It's not INDIVIDUAL
expression
and that's what
makes it so
WRONG.

GALACTIC EMPIRE

HELL END THE REBELLION ⊛ ENLIST TODAY!

We get some of our jobs from Vizago and the Broken Horn syndicate. He's a Devaronian crime boss active on Lothal, but he's no fan of the Empire. You can't always pick your allies, I guess.

Anyway, Vizago has a squad of IG-RM assassin droids as bodyguards.

Pretty deadly operators.

And I know Vizago is the kind of person who understands the power of a symbol.

Take another look at the Broken Horn's icon, right here.

That's why it drives me crazy that Vizago thinks it's okay for his enforcer droids to look so... BLEH!

SABINE WREN

I LOVE MUSIC.

Music is like painting, but for your ears.

MUSIC is about CREATIVITY, emotion, and sharing something with someone else. No wonder the Empire wants to stop it!

Musical scales are based on mathematics—the chords, intervals, tones, and rhythms, they're like a language all their own! And the best part is, it's a language that's universal to all music lovers no matter what planet they come from.

Music is **REAL** and **RAW**.

It's the voices of people sharing your troubles and your joys.

A few of my favorite listens over the last couple weeks:

- Verpine choral arrangements. They don't sing, they just rub their legs together!

- Phanuel, a new artist active in the Mon Calamarian diaspora scene

- Counterpunch/Kickback. Really the whole Core Drive sound in general

- Quenk jazz, especially Kain Apollyon and Mooneyes

- A rare recording of the Vors Concert of the Winds, supposedly dating from a couple centuries ago

Some nights in my cabin I slip on my helmet and activate playback, and within seconds my head is bathed in music.

Anatomy of an art hit!

ARTIST: Sabine Wren, Lothal
TARGET: TIE fighters docked groundside
MEDIUMS: Detonators, paint sprayer, adhesives

Here's how I pulled this one off!
(Recorded while the details are still fresh):

The rest of the crew needed a diversion. They needed the Empire's attention far away from their operations. And I'm great at diversions—especially whenever I make TIE fighters topple!

The landing field was surrounded by a sheer wall. I needed to get inside the compound but I didn't want the hiss of my jet pack to tip off the Imps - so I scaled the wall using cliff-climbing techniques!

Check out this pic Kanan took!

Once I got on the ground I planted explosives on a TIE and painted the wing with a purple starbird. An artist always signs her masterpieces!

Stormtroopers interrupted me before I could add the beak. I gave them the runaround—it's easy to hide in a forest of starfighters!—and circled back around so I could add the finishing touch.

I used the blinking detonator as starbird's eye. And when the whole thing blew sky-high, a knot of iron filings I'd packed into the explosive package glittered within the blast's contours. It looked just like a twinkling eye!

Here's the result!

SEE WHAT I MEAN?

I like to sign my work using a starbird. It means "Sabine was here," but only to me.

I designed the look of it, but I took inspiration from the old legend.

There's a lot of meaning to the symbol.

According to some, the starbird can never die— whenever it seems to be gone, it's actually renewing itself in the heart of a nova.

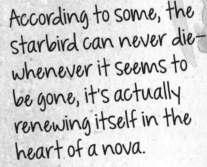

Starbird = ᛝᗡᐯᒋ (HOPE)

That's what we're fighting for. We're going to restore the spirit of the Republic. Unlike the tyrants of the Imperial regime, the elected leaders of the Republic tried to represent all people fairly and equally.

By giving the Republic a second birth we can make it even better than it was before! Every time the Empire sees the starbird it will give them something to think about. And something to be SCARED about!

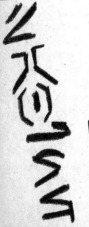

For the people of Lothal, this is a symbol they can **rally** around.

The Empire has outlawed free expression. What does that mean for artists? Commandant Aresko and officials like him don't realize that they've turned graffiti into the strongest artistic medium of them all.

Graffiti is art by the people.

It's public, and often anonymous. Some of it is just an artist saying "I was here," and that's okay! People want to be noticed and remembered.

And no one has the right to silence expression. Not even the Empire!

Sometimes graffiti can appear as beautiful, detailed murals. They're my favorites because I can tell the artists had the time to finish their vision.

REBEL!!

Here's some images of murals I shot around Capital City.

Why don't **THESE** artists have their work hanging in galleries?

Sometimes graffiti can be a warning. You see the Broken Horn symbol painted in alleyways, but it's probably just small-timers trying to scare people away. I doubt Vizago would bother with that stuff.

REBEL

This week we picked up a new stray: EZRA BRIDGER. He's a Lothal kid!

Ezra has been living on his own for a while and fighting the Empire in his own way. I like his spirit. He doesn't want to talk much about his past. But hey, neither do I.

He seems pretty good in a fight and he knows a lot about Lothal operations. When we planned a raid to free Wookiee slaves from an Imperial transport, we brought Ezra along. But then Zeb— such a vacuum brain sometimes, I SWEAR— left him behind when we had to escape!

We went back and got Ezra, of course. But come on, Zeb! Is that any way to treat family?

So the transport raid may have run into a few snags, but in the end it turned out to be another beautiful art hit! Chopper and I had orders to cut the transport's artificial gravity, so we snuck into the grav control station. I **could** have just packed a bunch of explosives into that chamber, but why be boring?

Instead, I brought along my pre-packed "special delivery" cargo and a customized detonator sequence.

MY OWN RECIPE

When they exploded, it looked like THIS!

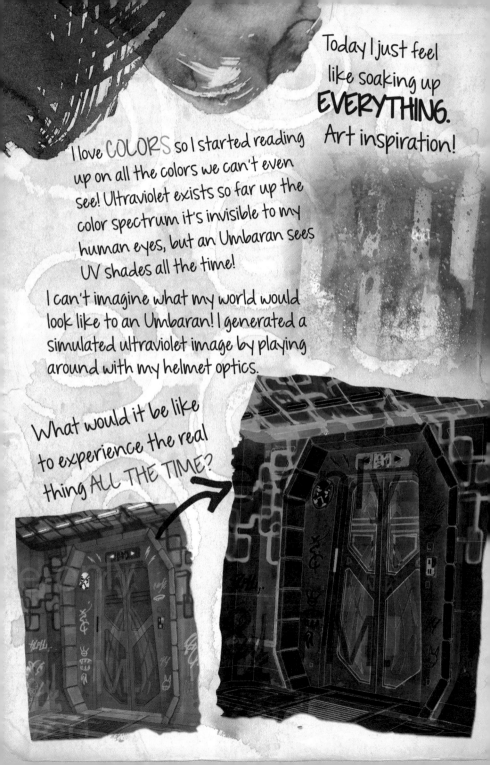

Today I just feel like soaking up **EVERYTHING.** Art inspiration!

I love COLORS so I started reading up on all the colors we can't even see! Ultraviolet exists so far up the color spectrum it's invisible to my human eyes, but an Umbaran sees UV shades all the time!

I can't imagine what my world would look like to an Umbaran! I generated a simulated ultraviolet image by playing around with my helmet optics.

What would it be like to experience the real thing ALL THE TIME?

AMAZING OLD CLAY!

In the corner of my cabin is a sticky pile of Lothal delta clay. I'm still deciding what to make out of it. I've had dried clay on my cheeks and nose for two days.

And I LOVE it!

Overheard on the shadowfeeds: moss painting is a big deal on Alderaan. It takes weeks to grow, but the patterns and colors of the different strains of moss can be amazing.

I **could** just lay down pre-grown moss patches using an adhesive growth culture. Hera might not like it, though—having strange plants aboard the Ghost, I mean.

And the Alderaan art purists would say my method is cheating. Do I care though? I really, **really** want to recreate a Jaynor of Bith canvas. But with moss!

Ezra's part of the crew now.

Meet Spectre-6!

That's great as far as I'm concerned. It's impossible for a family to be too big.

EZRA

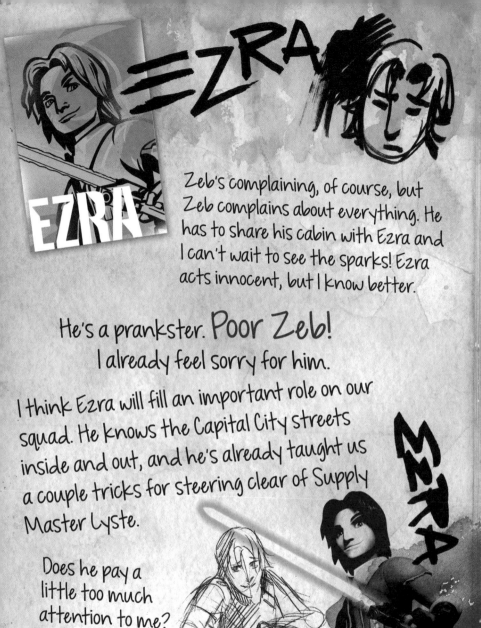

EZRA

EZRA

Zeb's complaining, of course, but Zeb complains about everything. He has to share his cabin with Ezra and I can't wait to see the sparks! Ezra acts innocent, but I know better.

He's a prankster. Poor Zeb! I already feel sorry for him.

I think Ezra will fill an important role on our squad. He knows the Capital City streets inside and out, and he's already taught us a couple tricks for steering clear of Supply Master Lyste.

Does he pay a little too much attention to me? Sure. But he's like, fourteen? I'm sure he'll grow out of it.

I'm liking sticker art more and more lately.

Stickers are easy to reproduce, and even easier to apply.

Not everybody in Lothal is an artist, and that's okay

JOIN THE REBELLION

FREEDOM FIGHTERS

JEDI USE THE FORCE

JUSTICE

If I print up a few HUNDRED anti-Empire slogans/ images on stickers and then I distribute them anonymously in the heart of Capital City...

Before you know it, these will be showing up EVERYWHERE!

(They're also really, really hard to remove once they've been plastered onto the walls of the government center!)

I LOVE languages!

There are so many ways to express the same basic ideas. Like love, family, and hope. Some concepts are universal, no matter where you come from or what you look like.

When you learn a few phrases in another language it's like getting inside someone else's head. It's good to get out of your own head once in a while!

I pick up languages pretty quickly. Back before I ditched the Imperial Academy, I was the fastest cadet to complete the language unit during espionage training.

So far, I speak Mando'a and Basic...

...and Huttese, and Aqualish, and Rodian—those three share certain structural similarities, so if you learn one you can learn the others...

A little Wookiee (but it's rough on my throat, I lost my voice for a day after bugging Zeb by serenading him in Shyriiwook)

I understand astromech droidspeak too. And I know I'm forgetting a few...

JEE OTO VO BLASTOH – I will keep my weapon

JE STOPYA UM PASA DOE BEESKA WUMPA – Stop me and ten more will rise in my place

VA VA VOOMEN FEST
VOM ZOOMEN FEST

KOPOCKA LOCKA HATTA STATA

SHYRIIWOOK
NUMBER STRUCTURE:
One: Ah
Two: Ah-ah
Three: A-oo-ah
Four: Wyoorg

So we just finished up the Garel job. **I had fun!**
Before the Imperial firefight, that is.

We needed to steal a cargo of disruptors from a spaceport on Garel, but to keep the **buyers** of that cargo away from the heist I needed to distract them. No, not with explosives this time!

WATCH OUT

On the shuttle ride over from Lothal to Garel, we took Minister Maketh Tua's translator droid out of the picture so she couldn't communicate with her Aqualish contact. I volunteered to translate, presenting myself as a good little Level 5 Academy student. So what if I mistranslated "Bay Seven" as "Bay Seventeen"? Easy mistake! Minister Tua didn't need to know that I got the details wrong on purpose.

I kept up appearances for the whole trip. What can I say? I'm a PERFORMER!

SABINE WREN

When Minister Tua figured out what we were up to, we had to deal with a squad of Imperial stormtroopers. And somehow, the two droids serving the minister got brought aboard when the Ghost blasted off from Garel.

C-3PO and R2-D2, I think. I liked the little astromech a lot.
Don't tell Chopper.

To escape from an ambush, we destroyed the entire cargo of T-7 ion disruptors. We lost a lot of money, but T-7s are bad news.
I'm happy we got rid of them.

The Empire has a monopoly on the media, and it's **got to STOP!** Under Imperial law, all businesses on Lothal are required to broadcast a continuous Imperial Holonet feed. It's pure propaganda but we can turn their tools against them.

You know who's got it all figured out? Senator-in-exile Gall Trayvis. He breaks into the Imperial feed with a pirate signal a couple times each week. When the Empire detects the intrusion they shut him out fast. But before they do, Trayvis gives people a concentrated dose of the TRUTH.

JAM ANY SIGNAL!

There are **so many ways** the Empire lies to people! I started picking up on this when I attended the Academy, and since then I've learned it's even worse than I thought.

FREE SPEECH

That "Base Delta Zero" initiative the Empire keeps talking about? The new "key to planetary liberation"? Don't believe it. It's a military code phrase, and it means TOTAL EXTERMINATION OF A TARGET POPULATION.

It's completely loathsome.

THE HOLONET

WANTED

APPROACH WITH CAUTION

GENDER:
  MALE
WEAPON:
  SIGNAL JAMMER

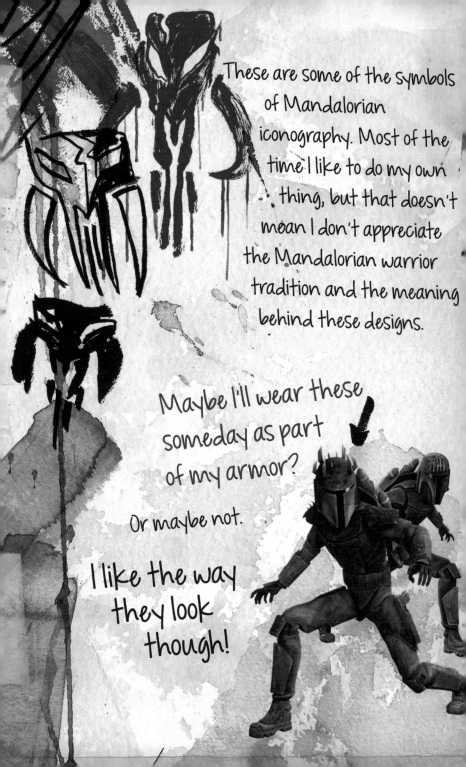

These are some of the symbols of Mandalorian iconography. Most of the time I like to do my own thing, but that doesn't mean I don't appreciate the Mandalorian warrior tradition and the meaning behind these designs.

Maybe I'll wear these someday as part of my armor?

Or maybe not.

I like the way they look though!

The Mandalorian cubist style went through a popularity resurgence during during the Clone Wars. I like this composition, but I hate how the artist's intention has been distorted by people in power. In this image I see a CONDEMNATION of war, **NOT** a celebration of it.

THE MANDALORIAN ART GALLERY

This morning, Ezra and Zeb were fighting again. I was getting pretty tired of it but Chopper was even more annoyed.

He finally decided to do something.

Chopper wheeled into their cabin and secretly loosened the fasteners on Ezra's top bunk. If you didn't know what he'd done you'd never have noticed the difference (Ezra didn't!). Basically, once he was done that bunk couldn't support anything heavier than a couple of pillows.

So of course Ezra flops down on it at the exact moment Zeb is trying to take a nap. Top bunk collapses on lower bunk! Zeb goes nuts, Ezra looks petrified, and Chopper rolls away going buzz-buzz-buzz like he does whenever he's really laughing.

Chopper

I've got to give the little droid some credit.

One of the **BEST** pranks I've ever seen!

CHOPPER

The whole thing was just too funny.
I knew I had to memorialize it immediately.

So when those two rock-heads left to make a supply run,
I made good use of a few hours of peace and quiet.

I have to create a mural of this!
I'll paint it on the cabin bulkhead. Heres a sketch.

Here's what I am thinking for color, something like this.

Ok I better get started on the real thing!
Can't wait to see their reaction to the unveiling!

MORE art inspiration!

The natural world is AMAZING.
I don't pay attention to it as much as I should.
Look at animals—they don't care about
governments or wars. We could learn
a lot from them!

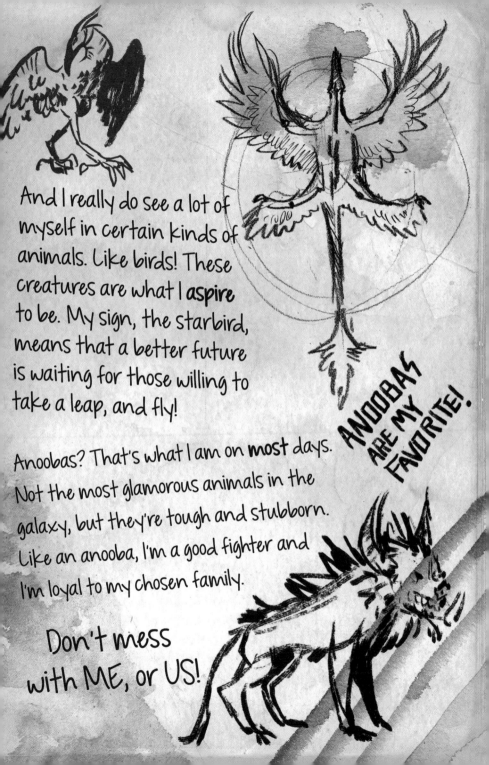

And I really do see a lot of myself in certain kinds of animals. Like birds! These creatures are what I **aspire** to be. My sign, the starbird, means that a better future is waiting for those willing to take a leap, and fly!

Anoobas? That's what I am on **most** days. Not the most glamorous animals in the galaxy, but they're tough and stubborn. Like an anooba, I'm a good fighter and I'm loyal to my chosen family.

Don't mess with ME, or US!

ANOOBAS ARE MY FAVORITE!

This is STYGEON PRIME:
home of the Spire. It's SUPPOSED to be an
escape-proof prison.

That was before we heard a
Jedi Master was locked up
in there: Luminara Unduli.
Somebody important during
the Clone Wars, Kanan said.
He met her once, years ago,
and believed she could really
help our cause.

We had to free her.
We had to **TRY**.

I sliced into classified building records to get the Spire's
hologram schematic so we could plan our op. This place
has it all: ray shielding, blast-proof walls, guard posts,
searchlights, scanners, heavy anti-ship weapons, and
TIE squadrons on scramble alert.

Hera and the Phantom dropped us off—me, Kanan, Zeb, and Ezra—on the sentry platform. I was hoping this whole raid could be completed stealthily, using Ezra's droid arm safecracker to disable the locks and my computer decryptor to get into their network.

But the Jedi prisoner had been moved to the lower levels, so we changed plans and went down. Zeb and I guarded the turbolifts. Kanan and Ezra headed off to Luminara's cell.

The instant the Empire jammed our comlinks, I KNEW the whole thing was a trap. Kanan and Ezra ran back to join us, the Inquisitor hot on their tails.

We got out, somehow. Past the stormtrooper patrols guarding the landing platform. Past the security-sealed blast doors. Past the Inquisitor and his spinning lightsaber.

Luminara might be gone, but that doesn't mean we failed in our mission.

We proved that even the best Imperial security CAN be cracked. That's something!

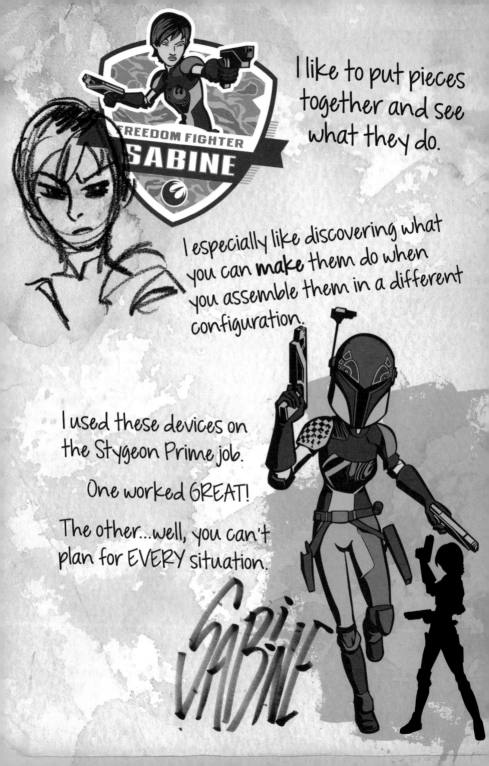

FREEDOM FIGHTER
SABINE

I like to put pieces together and see what they do.

I especially like discovering what you can **make** them do when you assemble them in a different configuration.

I used these devices on the Stygeon Prime job.

One worked GREAT!

The other...well, you can't plan for EVERY situation.

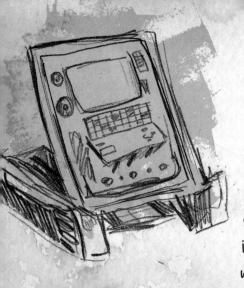

This is my decryptor. It's a brute-force computer slicer that beats most security systems but leaves a messy electronic trail. It's good for quick jobs, like pulling up classified schematics or splicing in fake security cam images, but not the best if you want to cover your tracks.

I knew we wouldn't be in the Spire long, so I took my chances with it.

And here's my scanner jammer.

It disrupts surveillance and control signals inside a two-kilometer radius (even farther under good atmospheric conditions).

On the Stygeon job, this thing accidentally emitted a sonic pulse that doubled as a mating call for a flock of tibidees.

JAM ANY SIGNAL

WHOOPS!

I want to get better at moving without being seen. I'm good but I can improve, and I need to be practically INVISIBLE if I want to keep making the Empire look stupid.

SABINE'S FIVE PRINCIPLES OF STAYING HIDDEN:

1.) Keep light on your feet. Don't make noisy steps.
Move quickly!

2.) Don't stay too long in one spot.

3.) Avoid lines of sight. If there's cover around, USE IT Stormtroopers don't have much peripheral vision in those helmets anyway.

4.) Climb fences and walls. Lots of entry points up there—they can't guard the whole thing at once!

5.) And never, ever get TOO CAUGHT UP IN YOUR ART! If an Imperial patrol is in the area I might not have much time. Maybe I can only throw up a couple of colors. I've got to remember to leave it where it is, and not blow the whole operation just so I can add the finishing touch.

Okay, easier said than done. I HATE seeing my vision go incomplete! I just keep telling myself: it doesn't have to be a masterpiece to be BEAUTIFUL.

STAY QUIET

YES! BOOM!!

REBEL

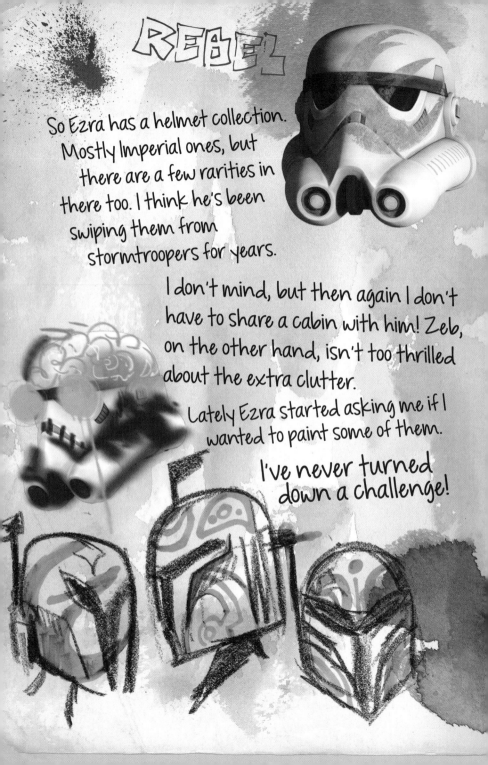

So Ezra has a helmet collection. Mostly Imperial ones, but there are a few rarities in there too. I think he's been swiping them from stormtroopers for years.

I don't mind, but then again I don't have to share a cabin with him! Zeb, on the other hand, isn't too thrilled about the extra clutter.

Lately Ezra started asking me if I wanted to paint some of them.

I've never turned down a challenge!

Here are some
ideas I'm
working on...

WHO IS FULCRUM?

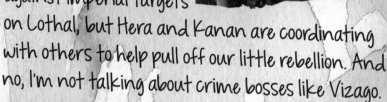

We keep making raids against Imperial targets on Lothal, but Hera and Kanan are coordinating with others to help pull off our little rebellion. And no, I'm not talking about crime bosses like Vizago.

Fulcrum is the code name for one of Hera's contacts, and apparently he's been supplying intel to us for a while. But when I asked her to explain, she said the details were on a "need to know" basis.

HERA

Hey Hera?

Guess what:

I NEED to KNOW.

I don't like being kept in the dark. Back at the Imperial Academy on Mandalore, I thought I should follow orders and never ask questions. That didn't end well. I'm not going to make the same mistake again.

I love Hera, but I'm getting frustrated. Kanan and Zeb might be happy just making headaches for the Empire, but I need more than that.

She says it's for everybody's safety. She says I need to trust her.

But SHE'S not trusting ME!

DOWN WITH THE EMPIRE!

DOWN WITH THE EMPIRE!

DON'T BELIEVE THE HYPE!

Shock and anger are negative emotions, but negative emotions can have a positive effect.

I KNOW that exposing the Empire's lies will fuel the people's desire for freedom.

Right now people are afraid.

Fear = inaction.

That's what the Empire wants.

But if we can turn fear into FURY, the people will demand change. They won't sit still and do what the Empire tells them. They'll join us in our fight! They'll become rebels too!

Maybe THEN we'll have a revolution here on Lothal.

And after that? THE GALACTIC CAPITAL!

DOWN WITH THE EMPEROR

i DIDN'T VOTE FOR HiM!

REBELS RULE

DOWN WITH THE EMPIRE

I love **making** art, and that sometimes means applying art to myself!

I've been keeping my hair short because it gets really sweaty under that helmet. Don't know if I want to trim it more or even go close-scalp shaved? Maybe? It's not like it won't grow back.

Hair by Sabine

I LOVE THIS ONE! CUTE! SHORT! BREEZY

HALF SHAVED & 2-TONED

Dye jobs could be fun. I read about this Mon Cal microplankton you can wash into your hair, where it bonds with each strand and emits a pulsating, bioluminescent glow. I'd love to try that, but don't think it would be a good match with nighttime stealth missions.

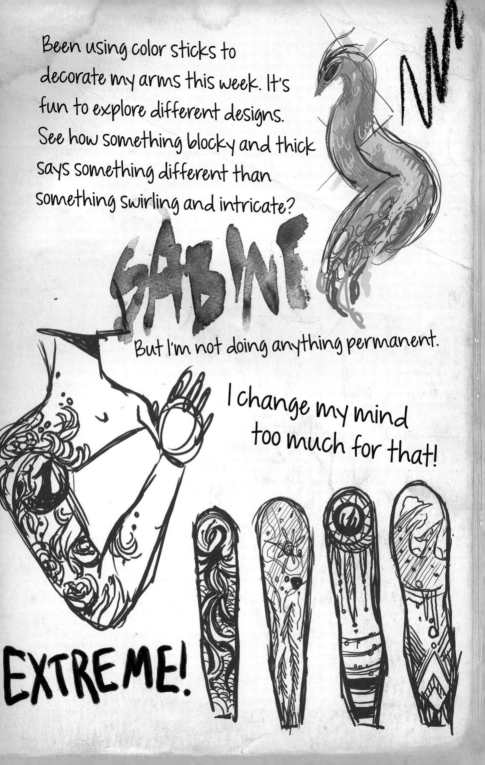

Been using color sticks to decorate my arms this week. It's fun to explore different designs. See how something blocky and thick says something different than something swirling and intricate?

SABINE

But I'm not doing anything permanent.

I change my mind too much for that!

EXTREME!

Today I finally got fed up with Hera keeping secrets from me - the ones about Fulcrum and everything else in this operation.

When she said she needed to take the Phantom to make a supply run **I invited myself along.**

Our mission was to rendezvous at an abandoned asteroid base and pick up cargo that Fulcrum had left for us. I don't know what I was expecting, maybe to confront Hera's contact and get some answers. But when we arrived the place was deserted, except for the cargo.

Or at least that's what it looked like. When we started loading up the supplies, I learned why this base had been empty since the Clone Wars.

Fyrnocks.

Bad-tempered things, with sharp teeth for gnawing minerals from rocks—or for chewing **on our bones,** which is what a pack of them decided to do after they burst from the shadows!

A fuel leak meant we couldn't escape on the Phantom. Ezra and Zeb were supposed to fix that!

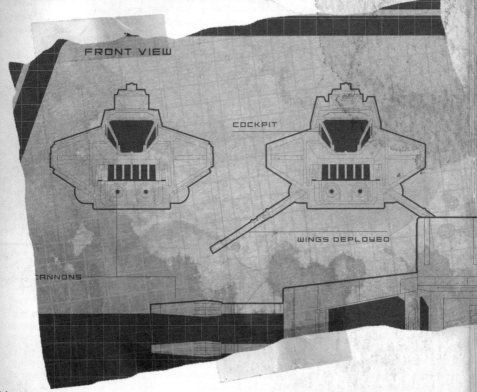

FRONT VIEW

COCKPIT

WINGS DEPLOYED

CANNONS

Hera and I held them off long enough for the Ghost to come to the rescue. And when we were fighting side by side, I realized that Hera trusts me with her life.

Looking at things in that light, I guess I can **trust** her with a FEW details of mission security.

There's SO MUCH to see in the galaxy!

I finally went through all the files I've captured on my holo-imager. I've got thousands of images, going back months and months. We've visited a lot of planets! I've met a lot of people and I've seen ugliness and beauty in equal amounts.

I'm going to try to categorize all my images so I can search through them if I need art reference. Or whenever I'm hungry for emotional motivation.

The Empire has a
Five-Year Plan for Lothal,
and it's not good.

TSEEBO

How do I know? Meet Tseebo—
or rather, meet the computer
on his head. Tseebo is fully
loaded with all kinds of
Imperial secrets, and sadly all
that data has done a num-
ber on his brain. He acts more
like a droid than a Rodian.
Luckily, we got Tseebo off
Lothal and safely into rebel
hands. I hope they can
help him.

We ran into Tseebo because we were in
Capital City to take part in the yearly
festivities that honor Emperor Palpatine
and his forced imposition of Imperial rule.

So how **DO** we celebrate Empire Day?
WITH EXPLOSIONS!

EMPIRE DAY

I had Zeb lob a few detonators up in the air as distractions so Kanan could get close enough to sabotage a shiny new TIE fighter prototype. Everybody thought it was a fireworks show. Told you explosions can be BEAUTIFUL!

I'm feeling pretty bad for Ezra after this mission. Seeing Tseebo brought up a lot of old memories for him. Ezra acts like he wants to forget the past, but I took some time to decrypt and restore an old data disk that he recovered. On the disk was an image of his parents, back before they disappeared.

I'm happy he has it, and I think Ezra is too.
Family is important.

I've got my family right here on the Ghost. I know in time Ezra will realize that too.

REBELS
RULE

SABINE
WREN

I SHOULD
USE THIS ON MY ARMOR!

Out of room already?

When I reach this point, I'll know it's time for
me to start another sketchbook. Here's to
new inspirations and new adventures!

— SABINE WREN

Writer: Daniel Wallace
Editor: Benjamin Harper
Illustrator: Annie Stoll
Art Director: Andrew Barthelmes
Designer: Gretchen Schuler-Dandridge
Copy Editor: Jay Gissen
Managing Editor: Christine Guido
Creative Director: Julia Sabbagh
Associate Publisher: Rosanne McManus
Lucasfilm Editor: Jennifer Heddle
Lucasfilm Story Group: Leland Chee, Pablo Hidalgo

Published by Studio Fun International, Inc.
44 South Broadway, White Plains, NY 10601 U.S.A. and
Studio Fun International Limited,
The Ice House, 124-126 Walcot Street, Bath UK BA1 5BG
 Printed in China.
Conforms to ASTM F963
10 9 8 7 6 5 4 3 2 1
SL2/09/14

VA VA VOOMEN FEST